For Michael and Scott,
lovers of history—C.F.

To my son Eric—R.A.P.

The HATMAKER'S SIGN

A STORY BY BENJAMIN FRANKLIN

Retold by Candace Fleming • *Illustrated by* Robert Andrew Parker

ORCHARD BOOKS • NEW YORK

At last!

After endless hours of scribbling and struggling, Thomas Jefferson had written it. And it was perfect. Every word rang. Every sentence sang. Every paragraph flowed with truth.

"It is exactly right," Jefferson exclaimed. "The Continental Congress will surely love it."

But the next morning, after Jefferson's wonderful words had been read aloud, the Congress broke into noisy debate.

"I do not like this word," quibbled one delegate. "Let's replace it."

"And this sentence," argued another. "I think we should cut it."

"What about this paragraph?" shouted still another. "It must be removed!"

While the Congress argued around him, Thomas Jefferson slumped into his chair. His face flushed red with anger and embarrassment.

"I thought my words were perfect just the way they were," he muttered to himself.

Just then he felt a consoling pat on his shoulder. He looked up and into the sympathetic eyes of Benjamin Franklin.

"Tom," Benjamin Franklin said, smiling, "this puts me in mind of a story."

In the city of Boston, on a cobblestoned street, a new hat shop was opening for business.

All stood ready. Comfortable chairs had been placed before polished mirrors. Wooden hatboxes were stacked against one wall. And the front window was filled with tricorns and top hats, coonskins, and wool caps.

There was only one thing the hat shop did not have—a sign.

But the hatmaker, John Thompson, was working on it.

Knee-deep in used parchment and broken quill pens, John struggled to create a sign for his shop. And at long last, he wrote one. It read:

Beneath the words, John drew a picture of a hat.

"It is exactly right," John exclaimed. "Customers will surely love it."

But before hurrying to the sign maker's shop, where his words and picture would be painted onto board, John showed his parchment to his wife, Hannah.

"Oh John," Hannah giggled after reading what John had written. "Why bother with the words 'for ready money'? You're not going to sell hats for anything else, are you? Remove those words and your sign will be perfect."

"You're probably right," sighed John.

So John rewrote his sign. Now it read:

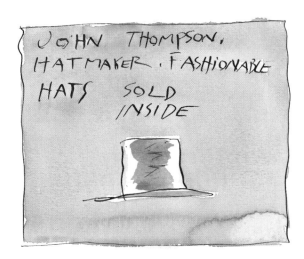

Beneath the words he drew a picture of a hat.

Parchment in hand, John headed for the sign maker's shop.

He had gone as far as the Old North Church when he met Reverend Brimstone.

"Where are you strolling on such a fine morning?" asked the reverend.

"To the sign maker's shop," replied John. He held out his parchment.

Reverend Brimstone read it.

"May I make a suggestion?" he asked. "Why don't you take out the words 'John Thompson, Hatmaker'? After all, customers won't care who made the hats as long as they are good ones."

"You're probably right," sighed John.

And after tipping his tricorn to the reverend, John hurried back to his hat shop and rewrote his sign. Now it read:

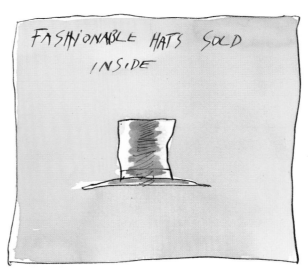

Beneath the words he drew a picture of a hat.

Parchment in hand, John headed for the sign maker's shop.

He had gone as far as Beacon Hill when Lady Manderly stepped from her carriage and into his path.

"What have you there?" asked the haughty lady. She plucked the parchment from John's hand and read it.

"Absurd!" she snorted. "Why bother with the word 'fashionable'? Do you intend to sell unfashionable hats?"

"Absolutely not!" cried John.

"Then strike that word out," replied Lady Manderly. "Without it, your sign will be perfect."

"You are probably right," sighed John.

And after kissing the lady's elegantly gloved hand, John hurried back to his hat shop and rewrote his sign. Now it read:

Beneath the words he drew a picture of a hat.

Parchment in hand, John headed for the sign maker's shop.

He had gone as far as Boston Common when he met a British magistrate.

The magistrate, always on the lookout for unlawful behavior, eyed John's parchment.

"Hand it over or face the stockades!" demanded the magistrate.

John did. He gulped nervously as the magistrate read it.

"Tell me hatter," bullied the magistrate. "Why do you write 'sold inside'? Are you planning on selling your hats from the street? That is against the law, you know. I say delete those words if you want to stay out of jail. And if you want your sign to be perfect."

"Yes, sir. No, sir. I mean I will, sir," stammered John.

And after hastily bowing to the magistrate, John hurried back to his hat shop and rewrote his sign. Now it read:

Beneath the word he drew a picture of a hat.

Parchment in hand, John headed for the sign maker's shop.

He had gone as far as the Charles River when a brisk breeze snatched the parchment from his hand and dropped it at the feet of two young apprentices sitting on a crate of tea.

The first apprentice picked up the parchment and read it.

"Hey, mister," he said. "Why do you write 'hats' when you already have a picture of one?"

"Yes, why?" asked the second apprentice.

"It would be a much better sign without that word," suggested the first apprentice.

"It would be perfect," added the second apprentice.

"You are probably right," sighed John.

And after tossing each boy a halfpenny, John hurried back to his hat shop and rewrote his sign. Now it read:

Nothing.

He drew a picture of a hat.

Parchment in hand, John headed for the sign maker's shop.

He had gone as far as Harvard College when he met Professor Wordsworth.

John shoved his parchment under the professor's nose. "Please, sir," he said. "Would you tell me what you think of my sign?"

The surprised professor straightened his spectacles and peered at the picture.

"Since you ask my opinion, I shall give it," said Professor Wordsworth. "However, I must ask you a question first. Are you displaying your hats in your shop's front window?"

John nodded.

"Then this picture is useless," declared the professor. "Everyone will know you sell hats simply by looking in your window. Eliminate the picture and your sign will be perfect."

"You are probably right," sighed John.

And after pumping the professor's hand in thanks, John hurried back to his hat shop and rewrote his sign.

Now it read nothing.

It showed nothing.

It was wordless and pictureless and entirely blank.

Parchment in hand, John headed to the sign maker's shop.

Past the Old North Church and Beacon Hill. Past Boston Common and the wharf and Harvard College.

At long last, John arrived at the sign maker's shop. Exhausted, he handed over his parchment.

"I do not understand," said the puzzled sign maker as he stared at the empty parchment. "What does this mean? What are you trying to say?"

John shrugged. "I do not know anymore," he admitted. And he told the sign maker about his new hat shop, and his sign, and how no one had thought it was perfect enough.

When he had finished, the sign maker said, "May I make a suggestion? How about:

'John Thompson, Hatmaker

Fashionable Hats Sold Inside for Ready Money.'

"Beneath the words I will draw a picture of a hat."

"Yes!" exclaimed John. "How clever of you to think of it. That is exactly right! Indeed, it's perfect!"

"*So you see, Tom,*" concluded Benjamin Franklin. "No matter what you write, or how well you write it, if the public is going to read it, you can be sure they will want to change it."

For several moments, Thomas Jefferson pondered Franklin's story. Then sighing with acceptance, he listened as the Congress argued over the words that rang, the sentences that sang, and the paragraphs that flowed with truth.

And surprisingly, when the debate was done, and the changes were made, most believed Thomas Jefferson's Declaration of Independence was exactly right. Indeed, they thought, it was perfect!

Author's Note

During his lifetime, Benjamin Franklin was an inventor and statesman, scientist and printer, postmaster and patriot. He was also a grand storyteller.

Indeed, there was nothing Franklin liked better than to tell a good tale. And he told them all the time. With the words "this puts me in mind of a story," Franklin could make people laugh or cry. Or, as he did with "The Hatmaker's Sign," he also made a point.

The original version of this story can be found in *The Papers of Thomas Jefferson.* Wrote Jefferson: "Dr. Franklin perceived that I was not insensitive to Congress' mutilation of my document, and tried to reassure me by whispering a parable."

Obviously, Franklin hoped his story would soothe Jefferson's hurt feelings and help him understand that revision is simply a part of writing.

Did his story help?

Not really.

By the time the debate over the Declaration ended, members of the Continental Congress had made a total of eighty-seven changes to Jefferson's draft. They cut words, rewrote sentences, and in two places, removed entire paragraphs. Nowadays, most historians agree that these changes made the Declaration of Independence a stronger document.

But Jefferson never saw it that way. For the rest of his life he stewed over the changes. He sent copies of his draft to various people in hopes they would admit it was better. He complained bitterly about his fellow delegates' lack of literary style. And when he wrote his autobiography more than forty years later, he made sure to include his version of the Declaration with all the parts struck out by the Congress underlined in black. Still, Jefferson obviously took pride in drafting the document. On his deathbed in 1826, he listed the edited version of the Declaration of Independence as his greatest accomplishment.

As for Franklin?

He continued to tell his stories until his death in 1790. But perhaps the most memorable tale he ever told was of a hatmaker and his sign—a story to heal the hurt pride of the author of the Declaration of Independence.

Text copyright © 1998 by Candace Fleming. Illustrations copyright © 1998 by Robert Andrew Parker. First Orchard Paperbacks edition 2000. All rights reserved. No part of this book may be reproduced or transmitted in any form or by any means, electronic or mechanical, including photocopying, recording, or by any information storage or retrieval system, without permission in writing from the Publisher. Orchard Books, A Grolier Company, 95 Madison Avenue, New York, NY 10016. Manufactured in the United States of America. Printed and bound by Phoenix Color Corp. Book design by Mina Greenstein. The text of this book is set in 16 point Janson. The illustrations are watercolor paintings with black ink reproduced in full color.
Hardcover 10 9 8 7 6 5 4 3 2   Paperback 10 9 8 7 6 5 4 3 2 1
Library of Congress Cataloging-in-Publication Data. Fleming, Candace. The hatmaker's sign / by Candace Fleming ; illustrated by Robert Andrew Parker.   p.   cm.   Summary: To heal the hurt pride of Thomas Jefferson as Congress makes changes to his Declaration of Independence, Benjamin Franklin tells his friend the story of a hatmaker and his sign.
ISBN 0-531-30075-7 (trade : alk. paper) ISBN 0-531-33075-3 (lib. bdg. : alk. paper) ISBN 0-531-07174-X (pbk. : alk. paper)
[1. United States. Declaration of Independence—Fiction. 2. Jefferson, Thomas, 1743–1826—Fiction. 3. Franklin, Benjamin, 1706–1790—Fiction.] I. Parker, Robert Andrew, ill. II. Title. PZ7.F59936Hat 1998 [E]—dc21 97-27596